THAT NIG

TARA
DEAL

THAT
NIGHT
ALIVE

MIAMI UNIVERSITY PRESS

Library of Congress Cataloging-in-Publication Data

Names: Deal, Tara P., 1965- author.

Title: That night alive / by Tara Deal.

Description: Oxford, Ohio : Miami University Press, [2016]

Identifiers: LCCN 2016021932 | ISBN 9781881163602 (softcover)

Subjects: LCSH: Storytelling--Fiction.

Classification: LCC PS3604.E144 T48 2016 | DDC 813/.6—dc23

LC record available at https://lccn.loc.gov/2016021932

Designed by Quemadura

Printed on acid-free, recycled paper

in the United States of America

Miami University Press

356 Bachelor Hall

Miami University

Oxford, Ohio 45056

FOR DAN

For the first time, in that night alive
with signs and stars, I opened myself to
the tender indifference of the world.

ALBERT CAMUS
The Stranger

I write in order to live and I live in order
to write, and I've come close to imagining that
writing and living might merge completely.

GEORGES PEREC

THAT NIGHT ALIVE

ACCOUNT 34

DECEMBER 24

No. Now. A moment.

Of hesitation, as expected. I should have known.

I should have known better. I should have stopped a while ago, put a stop to things. Before things got to this point. But I want to write one more piece, a piece of something, something else, greater. I would like to tell the truth. To make some corrections.

But that's not going to happen, is it. This is the last wisp then. I've known for a while that today is my end. Tonight, that is. I've been watching the numbers shift on the clock, counting down, as if to New Year's Eve. But there is still this last sliver of existence to endure. See what there is to see at the last minute, when it all becomes transparent. Or obvious. I can't remember what they call it. Before my final failure.

The worst thing about this disease, or so they say, is that it has a deadline. The doctor can determine your exact time of death. (Paperwork can be filled out in advance. Plots can be arranged.) The press keeps reporting, repeating the stories. Confusion is to be expected.

3

But I'm not reading any more. The necessary pages have been destroyed.

The champagne has been poured. I have poured it myself. I remember when people used to drink on certain holidays, before the celebrations were suspended. The smell of excitement on the street.

But my windows are sealed. Icicles hang down in front. I look past them, into the city. This City of Dreams. A blurred sign seems Japanese. Sirens in the distance. I wrap a blanket, maybe velvet, around my shoulders in case of shock. I imagine fireworks.

Although the doctor has told me not to think like that. It will be as if someone flips a switch and all the lights of the city go off at once. All the lights of the world, in fact. You won't feel a thing. And isn't that what I've always wanted?

ACCOUNT 33

DECEMBER 20

I've always wanted to be objective, impersonal, and great. To do a good job and get it right. To produce something monumental but not out of marble. Not that kind of artist. I wanted to clarify the confusion of things. That was my directive. But I was responsible for my own work, that's what they said. Reports were to be self-corrected.

And now, the end. Almost, that is. And what have I done? I have done a bad job. Do they have any proof?

Either way: what have I done to prepare myself?

Because there is still time to consider suicide, as always.

Which is what I've always planned. But not like this. I thought I could pick my own death date and do it quietly, after certain things had been achieved. After something (not a novel, not any more) had been accomplished. After I had become accomplished.

I have pills and old red wine. (Enough?) And rope (which I wouldn't know what to do with). And one antique electrical device that can be dropped into a tub.

I will have to do it soon, given my condition.

In the meantime, I might do something else. There is still time. But no reprieve. Not one person, yet, has recovered from this disease.

I look out: darkness. With sparkle at the edges. Navy skyline, and I wonder: which dress? So many fabrics, some metallics.

And I am surprised by the luxury, frankly. I try to enjoy what I have before it's gone. That's what was suggested. The bathroom is spotless and cold green marble, which I would have never chosen for myself, obviously. The light fixtures are impossible to describe. The body potions in opaque brown bottles smell like orange rind.

I once knew someone who committed suicide and he was thoughtful enough to lay down a tarp first. But he had used a gun.

OCTOBER 1

He had used a gun? The doctor advises against old-fashioned weapons and suggests something else, less invasive. He tells me to go home and wait.

Outside, it is autumn, I think. The dates on which the seasons begin are always changing. No matter. Why bother. A blip in the brain even to think of it. Time is speeding up as I approach the end, as I had been told it would. Stop looking around the bend.

I have a friend (call him Jake) who, I thought, would save me. He seemed to have access to a stockpile of medicine rumored to do the trick. But he has not been able do anything for me. Not yet, but maybe. There are difficulties. Obstacles, he calls them. Plus, one has obligations. There are other people. So I make a list. Things to be done. Things I should do.

In order to prepare myself. That's what I keep hearing in the waiting rooms, in the elevators. Here's my chance to do it right. But.

I always thought I'd leave something behind. A body of work. A final, finished product. Wasn't that the point of everything? Or at least an epitaph. I was going to write that, at least, long ago, at the start, when I arrived in this city, but so far, I haven't. My plans have not worked out.

Tonight I will destroy my notes, my sources. Also, I don't want to cause any more trouble. That's what they told me.

I have instructions for how to get rid of everything. I will mangle or disintegrate, depending. They forced me to read the manual about how to proceed, and I fingerprinted each page to prove that I understood. I saw there was no mention of my personal work, my micro memoirs. What to do with them. A loophole, perhaps. I didn't ask.

Maybe they think I destroyed the nonfiction long ago, when I was supposed to.

The micro memoirs are useless to them, in any case. Not even an official genre. Scattered paragraphs, sometimes less. They look like just another romance or a mystery. To the interrogators and random readers. (It is the work for hire they are worried about.) The memoirs are just what I've always had, nothing to get excited about. Notebooks made out of paper, even, and falling apart. They won't last. Overfilled, over the years, with flashes of feeling, phrases to remember, playbills, ticket stubs, signs that life has been lived and one is so well-traveled. Paint chips of colors I have loved. Such stuff, too much. To burn, that is.

ACCOUNT 31

JUNE 20

To burn, that is, the skin, just a pinch. This is how the doctor explains it, the technique to diagnose my disease.

And then: wait a minute.

And then: I am given my expiration date. The doctor says I can put the rings back on my fingers. Although sapphires and black jade won't save me now. (Some people think they ward off evil spirits.)

He says that given my history, plus the time spent in Thailand and Fez, my disease should end on December 25. That's the date. Just a coincidence. It has nothing to do with Christmas, which might be on a different day this year.

I point out that I have been living most recently in Paris. I was there for some time. I have just returned home, here.

The doctor says, in that case, I can look back and figure out when everything began, when this disease was transmitted to me, even which evening. But now that it has started, it would proceed, regardless. So why bother with history and literature? But if I wanted, he could give me something to read.

Then he asks if I'd been targeted. Could someone have injected me? Maybe. I took subways and flew on commercial airplanes and did my own shopping, sometimes, rarely. If that's what he was asking, but it wasn't. What he meant was: did I have any enemies? I suppose. Perhaps they were smart enough not to reveal themselves to me. And the doctor admits that, yes, this is a good possibility. Given my line of work and so forth.

Although I have kept my work a secret from him.

He does not know about my reports. That I write reports to fill up the press, to fill up the cracks. I write reports so tiny that they are inescapable. They flicker into any, every attention span. My work is like perfume, slowly suffocating everyone in the room.

The doctor says he is sorry that he doesn't have any answers. But I haven't asked him any questions.

He reassures me that the species is not in trouble. Only the individual. But the individual is expendable, yes?

And the doctor apologizes immediately. He says something else about my death sentence. Another mistake. Not in front of a patient. But it's fine. It gives me an idea. Death sentence: time to write my last lines. Like an epitaph but not quite. Time to make an effort and do it right.

The Japanese have a tradition of writing a death poem before they leave this world. An ancient tradition, not something invented to deal with the current crisis. Really, the doctor says, how do you know that, although he is looking at one of his screens now and not at me. I spent some time in Tokyo. But the attendant has already opened the door to pull me out. So the doctor doesn't ask me when or why. Or why not, even.

He says he will see me again in the fall.

I think ahead to autumn. I try to remember. Windy streets, leaves blowing. The cold ocean.

PAINT CHIP

WISTERIA

The cold ocean—so baby blue, so true!—surrounds me on this island. No, the water is more like a river, two rivers, that is, and I
breathe it in, all the salt and sting. I have just arrived, finally, after
waiting for so long, and so I take a moment to feel the wind off
the water. Red leaves blow past shop windows filled with golden
bowls. Autumn, my favorite season, and a fresh start. There was
a writer I loved who kept a journal and in it he wrote that autumn
"is indeed a spring. All the year is a spring." But he is not my role
model, not really, not at all, but I have some of his books, along
with others, among my clothes not meant for winter. I am carry-
ing everything with me. But that's all right, and I feel sure that I
can manage, because this is it, my new beginning, my real life,
finally.

My first apartment is just a room with bars on the windows,
and although I can't see the water any more, not right now, I am
happy to be here, home. I am down near the ground, which is
not the most desirable level, I know. Because things can slip in
through the bars, through the cracks. There is always the chance
of an attack.

I imagine another apartment, a better place, something beautiful that will appear later. It will be part of an overall artful life, full of things like metallic wallpaper and old red wine and a white lacquered desk scattered with good work. There will be huge windows with views of the skyline and the river. That's what I imagine, things like that, success.

I write it all down, what I can, when I can, because it's nice to have a record.

I have nothing from my childhood, for example. Which was landlocked and seems like a story remembered by someone else, although I remember it, of course, sporadically, sometimes. I remember the waiting, waiting all the time, inside, with the air conditioning on, in my bedroom with the beige carpet and my plastic tea set while my father cut the grass on Saturday mornings. I remember waiting for something (beautiful) to happen, to begin. But it never did.

Someone gave me a puzzle so that I could entertain myself, but I wasn't interested in figuring out things like that if there was no prize. I wanted adventure and treasure. I longed for activities that required long black dresses and crystal earrings.

And now here I am, finally. Although I don't have any long dresses, not yet. I don't even have any closets. But that's all right, and at least I am here, existing in this city, the city of New York, where things can happen, the center of the world.

That's what I've read, that's what I said.

I am breathless, having just arrived.

The heat hisses, but I don't understand the system. I struggle to open the window, just a sliver. I run my hand along the walls, which are bumpy with things buried under the old paint.

I take out my stack of paint chips and wonder which color. Although no alterations are allowed within the apartment. Changes will cost you. But I've always taken as many paint chips as possible, as many as I could carry, because they are free, at least for now, and you never know what might happen, when you might need them.

Paint chips are one of my mnemonic devices, for remembering what living here is like.

I shuffle the colors, as if they were the cards of a fortune-teller. Maybe they will reveal my future and foretell my story. Although maybe not.

I look outside and see a woman in front of a newsstand. She takes off her gloves, just for a moment, to fondle the numbers on a lottery ticket, admiring the combinations. And she smiles, in love, good luck.

This autumn is colder than ever before.

The frozen sidewalk turns into a mirror, and a dog walks by in a mink coat.

I struggle to close the window, but it's too hard. Somehow, I will have to fill the gap.

JUNE 6

Fill the gap with distraction. This is what Jake advises. Don't worry about the future or the doctor. Pay attention to the present moment. That's all you have. I tell him that I don't know what he's talking about. Jake says he is sure that I am fine. And if not, he has a contact with access to certain potions, that's what he calls them. A medicine already in development. He could get his hands on it, maybe.

But it doesn't matter. That is, I've always been careful. When traveling. Avoiding ice in drinks and mango on streets. Never drink the bottled water without a seal. Never eat the catfish. I've tried to take it all in without exposing myself. To unnecessary risk.

I say these things. To make Jake feel better. Because it is his fault that I went to Paris. That I am now in this situation. It was Jake who recruited me. Although at the time, I thought he was doing me a favor.

And now I have been doing this work for so long, for how long. Getting paid as much as possible. I remember when I wanted it. This job in the field of crypto-reportage, which I had never heard of. But I thought it was my chance. I thought it would be worthwhile. To write messages that other people would read. Even though it wasn't exactly journalism. And I wanted to do a good job, of course. That's why I started. Although, even now, I am not allowed to tell anyone what my job is. I cannot explain what I do or did. So no one imagines that I've done anything. Except Jake, who laughed when I first met him, because he couldn't believe I was the person he'd been sent to get. When he asked about my experience, I mentioned the micro memoirs, what I wrote in my flat, and he was not impressed. That's not what you do to make a living, is it? No, of course not. Or, rather, yes. What I meant was something else.

ACCOUNT 29

JUNE 4

Something else has gone wrong inside my body. It feels like a spring has broken. Or a clasp has snapped. Something has happened. I am not immune. I know that.

The news reports are mapping the fresh outbreaks. They don't know what to say, what to call it. The disease is number 28. It is attacking the planet, erasing populations. Africa and Thailand, especially, as always. People don't have time to prepare themselves. There is no form of protection. You have to live where you are, with what you have. That's what flashes on the screens, between the lines of other stories. Don't make any sudden moves. Keep the windows closed. Put up bars if you have them.

I continue to watch what happens. I listen to the reports.

I see smoke engulf the skyline, periodically. This Opaline City is disappearing. Rubble is piling up. Although it hasn't reached my floor yet, not even close. I do not know if this is part of that, however.

I will have to leave soon. There's a funeral, unrelated to this outbreak. I have no choice. That's what I tell them, the people who brought me here, who guard me here.

They say I am not a prisoner.

Even so, I have to ask permission. It feels like quarantine. I try to remember my training. Use the memory devices to save your sanity if captured. Recite your stories. I retrace my routes, revisit the bazaars. I look back and try to figure out the spices used to disguise the brains baked in the tagine that I ate in that place that I could never find again in Morocco. I wonder where my souvenirs are, if I have any left. At least I still remember the names that recall the way things were: Paris, Kyoto, Acapulco.

Although Acapulco has disappeared entirely.

Would you have done things differently, if you'd known how things would turn out? That's one of the questions on the self-exam I have to take before visiting any doctor for a flash diagnosis. I do not answer it. I mark it as "not applicable." I record my symptoms. Check the boxes. Some loss of local color. Double vision. Especially when I try to read the signs. In the afternoons, on the subway.

PAINT CHIP

SPRING GREEN

On the subway, I read it, a warning: "In NYC, it is illegal to paint a real gun to look like a toy, and it is illegal to buy a toy gun that looks real."

On the sidewalk, springlike, chartreuse, I feel it again, a new beginning, then three teenagers. One pulls out a gun that looks like a toy. He tells me to hand over everything. (No.) I don't even stop walking. I look like I know where I'm going.

I stop to watch a man try to move his gigantic sofa into an apartment elevator, and it can't be done. The mover says you'll have to leave it at home. He means wherever it came from. The man says he loves this sofa. The mover says, move on.

I keep walking until I see the plastic sushi in a restaurant window, and then I stop to admire it, to want it, to dream of Japan, as I always have. Ever since I was small and read a book about it. That book, if I remember correctly, told the story of several sisters and their dolls and all the miraculous, miniature things involved.

Cradles from walnuts, lanterns from thimbles. Everything in the universe of that small novel seemed so precise and right. The girls' mother placed tiny ceramic teacups on an autumn windowsill. Outside was a rain of soft yellow leaves, maybe even gingko. Lacquer appeared later.

Life could be composed like a haiku every morning, every afternoon.

Couldn't it also be like that in New York?

I am still trying to figure it out, how things work here.

I keep walking, gathering, going, hoping. And I still want to go to Japan one day, eventually, before my time runs out. People say I have all the time in the world for things like that. No need to hurry, no need to worry.

But Japan won't last forever.

MAY 10

Japan won't last forever, according to the latest report. But Japan seems far and foreign. Not part of my world, not any more. Now that I am here. Back in the Final City, that's what they're calling it this morning.

People were surprised when I returned. They wanted to know where I'd been, what I had done. What was my reason for being? What was the secret to my success? I thought that I'd make up my story as I went along. Something to impress. And I wouldn't worry if things didn't fit together at the edges. The chronology might be off. But who would notice? Every attention span is limited. I could say anything I wanted.

There was once a poet whose work was just fragments on papyrus, and people loved that. I thought my transition would be fine. That people would believe anything.

People sent messages saying they thought I loved Paris. Why did I leave? They said I would miss the booksellers who had been eliminated from other countries. And what about the illegal oysters and black pearls.

I said it was my work. That took me away. That made me return.

I said several things.

But some people had more questions. What kind of writer was I, really? They never saw my name on anything. Which was part of my contract, although I couldn't say that. I couldn't even say that I had a contract. I lived in a world that was a secret.

What I described sounded like a cover story. For something else. But what?

And where did my money come from? How could I afford Paris, which was so much more expensive than before?

And now that I'm back, I live in the tallest tower. The height of my career. How is that possible?

I pretend not to hear the questions. When I meet new people, at the events, sometimes parties, that I am forced to attend, against my will. I used to fantasize, out loud, it seems, about writing something beautiful. But I put an end to that. That is, I signed an addendum declaring I was unfit to discuss art. So I try to focus. Laugh when I should. Deflect attention. That would be good. That's what they said I should do.

PAINT CHIP

CRIMSON

That's what they said I should do: get a good job and work hard, right from the start. The classic advice, still being dispensed upon graduation. Who knows if it's true.

But it's hard to get a good job here, to find exactly what to do. To figure out what you like and make a mark. I say sometimes that I am here, living in New York, because I want to be a writer, even though people say those days are over. Being a writer isn't glamorous anymore. Books are dead. Or dying, at least, that's what people tell me.

But I don't have to write something immediately, necessarily. Maybe I will wait and see what happens. Maybe there is plenty of time to figure it out. I have some small amounts of money, enough to get started, although I will have to supplement with odd jobs and found items, but that's all right because the streets are full of things.

I try not to worry because at least I am in New York. Where I've always wanted to arrive, ever since I first heard about it, once upon a time, and who knows how long ago that was now. I re-member all the fantasies and disasters. I hoped they would balance out, and I hoped I would be happy in a place like that, like this, right now.

One day, I would also like to live in Paris, but who knows if that's possible.

In the meantime, however, New York. It's where I am, believe it or not.

I make notes in the evenings about what's going on around me. I try to be a voyeur. Not every night, of course. Sometimes, I have other things to do. No, not really. I don't know why I said that.

In the afternoons, in any case, I walk down the sidewalks, trying not to follow the same route, hoping to find something new. Sometimes, I see things. Sometimes, not often, I buy brass jewelry when it's cheap on a table outside of a storefront. I keep an eye out for bargains. I keep an eye out for information. Yesterday, passing by a café with tiny tables scrunched together under an awning, I overheard a professor ask his student: could love of one's work equal love of a person? Could a monk with his manuscript be as devoted as that couple close together over there, under an umbrella? It was that hour when the air starts to turn purple (violet). Yes, of course, why not. That was the answer to the professor's question.

A body of work. A path and a practice. That's what I want. When will I have it?

But first I need to figure out how to live.

I think about a girl who was stabbed recently. I didn't know her, but I try to think of appropriate last words. Not for her, but for myself. (I like to plan ahead.) I can write that much at least, that's what I figure. It would be a start. But I can't think of anything. Only the quotes of other people. Like that bit of Shakespeare on Shelley's stone in Rome, and I wonder if I will ever see it. Has the cemetery been slated for demolition?

But I know that if I am going to have a proper ending, I need to figure out how to begin.

How to being. That's what I type onscreen before my sentence corrects itself.

How to live. It is a mystery.

I close the screen and turn back to paper. Of which I have a stockpile. Friends and relatives are always giving me imported paper and velvet-covered journals. Plus, it's dangerous to record things on devices, because nothing can ever be deleted, not really. I don't know what I was thinking.

I look out of my window in the middle of the night and see a big red bank sign. SAVE something, that's what it says. But what does it mean?

PAINT CHIP

SESAME

What does it mean? These scribbles on the walls of buildings. The fluorescent pink arrows spray-painted at the intersections. Orange cones in the road. Coded controls at various entrances. Skyscraper lights that turn blue or green in the evening, depending. I started trying to decipher it all immediately, upon arrival in New York City. But I was starving (not really). Which was just part of the struggle. That is, everyone had a story, something similar. Someone gave me a bagel one morning. So warm and steaming. I couldn't believe how soft and delicious. Things like that didn't exist where I grew up or went to school. But now I'd seen it, this cipher, a sign. An indication of things to come: there were things like this all over the world. Giraffes in the ruins of the Colosseum. Black magic lava beads in Athens. Imagine *croissants au chocolate* and *pain au raisins* inside the Osaka train station.

ACCOUNT 27

MAY 5

Inside the Osaka train station: the world's best croissants. I still experience the phantom smell in the morning. Even though I have been back here, back home, for some time. Long enough to know that I have to stop looking for croissants in the morning. Another item banned in this Chrysalis City.

I am still unpacking the boxes. It will take forever. Mementos of other places. Apartments and hotels. I am trying to remember what it was like. I am trying to remember how to live here, now.

Because people live differently, after the Terror and the Scare. There are new routines and schedules. Avoid being outdoors when it rains. Stay inside after midnight. That's when they do the spraying. Steer clear of cats.

From my apartment, I look out over the top of the city. I can see a large swath of neon teal river. I am lucky.

My space in the Tower is hard to believe.

I deserve it, someone explained. Consider it payment for services rendered. For services still to come: that's what they mean. Although I do not know what they want from me now.

What kind of work? I go out at night, when they order me to, to attend the required events. So that things appear normal. I wear jewelry and one long black dress. They insisted on charmeuse. But inside the apartment, nothing to do. I am told to wait. Don't do anything. We will see what happens. Things will make sense soon. That is, things will end. You can count on it, they said. They remind me that I am expendable. They make every situation sound sinister. But I try to enjoy my new apartment. Light and silence.

The sky shifts from purple to white. The subtractions of snow. The slow removal. No cobblestones. No curbs. No horns. Only blowing.

A blank space and plenty of time. To write something wild or great.

What I've been waiting for. All my life, I almost said. But they warned me not to do it. Remember the stipulations. Also ultimatums. Do I want to sacrifice what I have? What I have worked so hard to achieve? Which sounds like a threat.

I continue to write my micro memoirs, however. Because who cares. I write in the high-security escape room where they can't see me on the monitors. That's what I think. I use paper, sometimes pencil. I continue to record the world. Maybe useless. Maybe true.

The escape room reminds me of certain hotel suites. There is the sensation of possibility. I try to remember traveling. I think of ordering up something to be delivered. To compensate or to celebrate, I can't remember which. Maybe champagne. Although no one is going to bring me anything if I ring for it. There is a yellow button at my front door that says HELP, but when I ask the attendant downstairs what happens if I press it, he says: Nothing.

ACCOUNT 26

NOVEMBER 25

Nothing but emerald glass in every direction from my terrace.
The Tower seems so spacious after Paris. I will be happy to stay
here forever. That's what they tell me, so that's what I say, when
they ask if everything is satisfactory. Then I repeat it, louder, for
the recording devices.

I had thought I'd be working abroad for longer. And it wasn't
entirely my fault that things didn't work out. I did my best. I even
borrowed a small apartment from a friend, or rather an acquain-
tance, and thereby spared them that expense. Or so I thought,
at the start.

I was given guidelines about the work. But then I did the work
according to my own schedule, my own nature. Problems arose.
The back and forth still goes on. They are trying to figure it out.
What happened. Who is to blame. The truth is: I took advantage
of my situation. I traveled every weekend, whether they liked it
or not (they did not). But I always did my work and turned it in
on time. I even went to Japan. They could track me, but they
could not prevent me from leaving the country, not at that point.
Not if they wanted to continue certain operations. Also, they

liked for me to think that I had some power. The illusion of free will makes writers happy. It was part of their manifesto.

Once, however, my windowpane was broken by a flying brick. Maybe it was a warning. But maybe it was an accident. One evening was filled with violent weather.

PAINT CHIP

NACRE

Violent weather last night means extra sparkle this morning. All the windows of the world have been washed.

I go outside to see for myself. Also, I can't stay in my apartment all day because it is so small, some would even call if claustrophobic, like living in a box, almost. Plus, I need to work. I have to find something. Whatever resources I came here with will soon run out or have, almost. I have to support myself, somehow, I know that much. But I don't know what.

A crate of seashells for sale moves around the sidewalk. Conchs and whelks trying to feel their way back. Oysters clutch their pearls.

I am learning how to live in New York.

Other people have done it. Other writers have lived here, and I wander down their streets, near the river. Someone has put a quote from Melville into the façade of an old building that is slanting, shifting. "Circumambulate the city of a dreary Sabbath afternoon," it begins. Then continues.

Then uptown in the drizzle, I walk by a discarded cardboard box that says: Become your Dream. The message has been written in thick black marker. But the box is ripped, a little soggy. It will not even be a box for much longer.

NOVEMBER 4

It will not even be a box for much longer. My place in Paris. They are prepared to destroy my studio, my flat, my garret, whatever you want to call it. They call it a box, and I say it isn't even mine. I borrowed it. I say that life in a box is better than, but they say: Stop.

There is a delegation to escort me. From the airport to my new apartment, inside the Tower. Where they show me the security features. Then explain that I cannot leave without recording certain information. Also, I might have to ask permission. It depends on where I want to go. They say that all of these procedures will become routine. They say that everything will make sense soon. Certain things will become invisible, and I can live as I always have. I can continue.

They say that I am lucky to be here. In this City of Scenes.

They ask what I have in my bags. Nothing.

I ask if there are cameras in the apartment. They point out my zones of privacy.

I am left alone to figure out how the coffee machine works. It is morning. The ice shines outside. The coffee machine is built into the wall. They have left no instruction manuals behind. They can't take a chance. Text = risk. The coffee grounds are sealed and I have to initialize a screen in order to open them.

I am living under a new arrangement now. Although I haven't read the agreement. Not yet, but I will.

PAINT CHIP

CAPPUCCINO

Not yet, but I will, one day, drink café au lait from a thick bowl every morning. That's what I tell myself, that's what I believe, more or less. Instead of drinking regular old coffee at home, on my sagging kitchen chair. From a standard mug with lowfat (unreal) milk. I don't even take the time, usually, to cradle my cup and sip slowly while looking out of the window, through the bars, at the gray August light. Which is what the mornings must look like in Paris, right?

My view is of white bricks. The humidity seeps in. It feels like Florida. Have I ever been?

Will I one day linger in cafés in other countries? I dream of being a foreigner, with croissants. I fantasize about traveling. I imagine my future imagination.

But I wouldn't want to forever drink coffee out of a bowl.

MAY 1

I wouldn't want to forever drink coffee out of a bowl. That is my consolation. When they send me out of Paris. My detention period is over. I have to go.

They are forcing me to leave because they found out. Something. But who knows what. I wasn't researching the international situation and I had no interest in the impending disaster, but someone mistook me for an informant or correspondent. Whatever they want to call it. Even though my mission was entirely different. But they had their evidence. They thought I was a rebel. That I was fighting for something else. Also, someone saw that I regularly sat down on a bench in the middle of the city to record my impressions. Scenarios, vignettes. It's possible that I looked desperate.

Because I was tired. Of things, my work. I wanted something better. Nausea came over me, regularly. I was remembering, somewhat, what I used to think I would accomplish one day.

Sometimes, I stayed in the same spot all afternoon, which must have looked suspicious. I forgot about the surveillance tactics. How to avoid them. How to proceed.

Sometimes, I stayed still until evening. I forgot about the time. Even though I know that keeping track of time is one of the things that a prisoner must do in order not to go crazy.

I once saw a man talk to his dog while dragging it uphill, against its will. The man convinced the dog to continue, all the way to the top, where there was a patisserie.

I made a note.

Someone must have been watching. It must have looked like a secret code I was writing. Something so secret that even I couldn't decipher it. Not now, maybe later.

My employer is not happy.

APRIL 27

My employer is not happy. He has received the information/ confirmation that I will soon be taken away. Out of the country. Just as things are starting to get interesting. That's what he says. But I can't escape the verdict. I have made an impression. That is, I take an impression. In order to remember the architecture. Also the rain, the river. The things that exist everywhere but are different. I might write a book, but I don't mention this, of course, because my contract prohibits the production of future artworks based on my employment experience. In any case, I try to remember things. I take whatever I can get away with. To shore up existence on another continent. As if memories were bricks. As if the whole trip weren't a trick.

ACCOUNT 22

APRIL 13

As if the whole trip weren't a trick, that is, a joke, I go to the mustard store for a visit. I try to believe in my mission. But I am losing focus. That is, losing hope. I sometimes stumble on the cobblestones. I want to do a good job, but this assignment is not what I had been looking forward to. Long ago. Once upon a time. It is not what I imagined when I started. But I do it, of course. And the faster I write, the more money goes into my account. There are bonuses and supplements. Forbidden fruit and vintage jewelry, for example. Sometimes, loose stones.

At the mustard store, I overhear a story. Two people talking about a secret key and a famous courtyard. On one side of the courtyard, hidden by climbing roses, there is a doorway, or rather a portal. It sounds ridiculous, but I write it up. I put it in my piece about how mustard is still being made in the artisanal way, at this special location, only in Paris. I mention raspberry mustard and cognac mustard and truffle mustard and hazelnut mustard, but I need more. Local color. So I talk about the courtyard. I say the roses are yellow.

That's it. Hand it in. Always to the same man, not exactly an editor. I always meet my deadline. I usually get paid the same day. This time, however, he hesitates.

Soon enough, the authorities arrive and take me away. I am detained. But unharmed. I am put in a cell and a category. I try to explain. They say they have evidence of my dual life. There is more than one story.

In my defense, I point out that what I write is the easiest form of entertainment. This particular piece isn't even well-written. Not even suspenseful. I try to convince them. They can't be serious. I point out the lack of attribution for my quotes. The allusions that lead nowhere. The sentence fragments. The speculation. Nothing sustaining or sustainable.

Someone says this is the perfect form/format in which to transmit information.

Every reader can see between the lines. Connect the figments.

And wasn't I being paid more money than I ever expected? Yes. Which they take as my confession.

ACCOUNT 21

JANUARY 2

My confession: I am not celebrating the new year this year. There is something in the quality of the light that is worrisome. Maybe the air. A vague feeling of pestilence. Paris is turning from gray to charcoal. Slight fever in the evenings. And I am tired of my work, writing the same stories. With the embedded messages. There are several that are cycled through the system. Not my concern. But the location for each piece has to be different. The semblance of originality. I go to the odd rooms and corners of the city. I am in search of an independent spirit and the artisan. That's what they tell me. Look for the local color. But fuchsia, for one, has disappeared. I can't see it. Someone says I should see a doctor. But I refuse to go to one of the clinics for foreigners.

I am going nowhere. Rambling rather than traveling. I want a change, although I've been warned not to think like that. They give me more money to keep me quiet/happy. Isn't this the perfect arrangement/assignment? They say that when a man is tired of Paris, he is tired of life. Which doesn't sound right. And they don't understand things like sadness.

PAINT CHIP

PINK MARBLE

Sadness of August magazines: so thin, as thin as the women who read them would like to be. They are too insubstantial to settle down with. Too frail to help someone (me) get through the long weekend. Especially when the night is hot and slick perfumed pages become a problem. They offer a few phrases about satin shoes and basketweave clutches and pink cocktails before dinner, but not enough. What they deliver cannot even fill up the space of one small studio apartment, where someone must order in Chinese food to flesh out the evening. If she can afford it. But remember, soon magazines will arrive that are dense and rich, layered with chiffon and lipstick, food and wine, lacquer and fun. Butterscotch knits and red velvet. Soon magazines will come with the heft of heartfelt promises: September.

PAINT CHIP

COSMOS

September, with the smell of smoke and my love of New York. The afternoon is all yellow leaves blowing past the bars of my window. I look out and think ahead, imagining more colors, even ochre, and a future full of things, afternoons full of meaningfulness.

But in the meantime:

I am going to compose a proper epitaph, in advance, so as not to be dependent on despondent survivors. That's what I've decided. I have wanted to do this for a while, ever since I arrived, but so far I haven't.

Or maybe it's better to leave no stone behind—just a mark made elsewhere (leave no stone unturned). I can never decide. In any case, the best epitaph I've seen so far is that of the poet Conrad Aiken (location of grave: Bonaventure Cemetery, Savannah, Georgia, my hometown). His stone, which is a bench, which is nice, declares: Cosmos Mariner—Destination Unknown.

I haven't been down there in a while. Friends and relatives say they understand. They can't say if anyone remembers Conrad Aiken, however.

And I didn't tell them, but I decided something else recently, something that seems momentous although maybe it isn't, and I can't remember when exactly I came up with this idea, because so many things have been happening, but once I decided to write my own epitaph, it seemed sensible to kill myself as well, eventually. Not right now, of course, but later. After I've lived a good life and have something to show for it. I've picked a round number for my final age. I've even set the date, because I love the idea of a deadline. (Something to work toward, the final accomplishment.) It should be fine to die if one has lived well and written something great, I don't know what but it doesn't matter, because I would also be happy to produce something small but just right, fragmented but evocative. Think of Sappho's phrases on papyrus held together with the tiniest pieces of tape.

And so, I look forward to it, the end, the consolation of doing it right, the conclusion that wraps up everything, that makes sense of the story. I have an expectation of symmetry. The fulfillment of a destiny. The solution to a universal problem.

But before all that, plenty of life and things. There are things I want and things I want to get done, and I hope to be able to travel and think and read the old books, in which Mountolive moves through the mauve dusk, a damp heat, with the reek of jasmine. There will be time for indecision and revisions. And I will write, I will try, that is, to write something grand, something like a novel but better than that because art is more important than life, that's what I think.

ACCOUNT 20

NOVEMBER 24

What I think, what I hope is that this last series of essays will be finished before the holidays. Then I can do what I want. But first, I have to report. A trip to the dressmaker, the last of her kind. An investigation into what used to be called millinery. The umbrella museum and the weather station. Then the mustard store, later, maybe.

I go to the remotest places. Where I listen to people explain things called rituals and tradition. I write it down. I follow the guidelines that I was required to memorize upon arrival in Paris.

But I am unenthusiastic. Maybe bored.

Just do the work. That's what I am told.

But I want to write something fresh. But I don't say that, of course. I don't say what. I would like to start on something else. Before things start happening. Or falling apart. Either way. But I don't talk about my fears or plans. I don't want to cause the alarms to sound.

My employer doesn't want to hear about it, my personal problems. He doesn't want any variation in the vignettes. That's what he calls them. A hint of nostalgia is good for the people. He tells me what he needs, and I provide it. That's how it works. Revisions are limited. Do it right the first time. This is serious work. The word counts are so precise that sometimes the facts are warped to fit. But that's fine. That's how it is. That is, I have been doing this work for too long now. How many years? Who keeps track? I try to argue, occasionally, but I never win. I never get anywhere. I am stuck. Paris is my compensation, that's what they tell me, more than once. And Paris is beautiful, but.

I travel as much as possible.

I travel as far as possible. Despite the ban on border crossings, which doesn't apply to me, or so I say. I am almost a journalist. That's what I tell people. The people who check things. I say that I am looking for inspiration.

I am tired of my occupation. My confinement. I want a new assignment, something outside the field of crypto-reportage, but what else is there. Arrangements are not easy to make. That's what they say. And I am still forbidden to write for myself. That's not going to change. I could stop writing altogether, of course, and escape. But it has been made clear to me that writing = life. If I stop, I die. Although they did not say it like that, not quite.

But the new year should have some surprises in store: that's what my horoscope says. And why do I read such things? Out of desperation. Why do you read anything.

ACCOUNT 19

FEBRUARY 4

Why do you read anything? they asked me. The answer would ensure my employment in the correct division. They would then provide the content guidelines and the coordinates for locations of the stories. But the actual writing, word by word, would be my choice. I could refuse. But who could refuse the chance to go to Paris on an open-ended assignment? That's how it was presented to me. Did I have any family? Did I have any problems? No, of course not. Could I accept the kidnapping risk that came with a French position? I took it immediately, this opportunity. They warned me about the side effects of glamour and travel. But it didn't matter because I was going to be the Paris correspondent, that's what they called it. I would capture something. The feel and mood of a foreign city for American readers. For example. But it could be anything. I wouldn't know until I got there. They had rooms of other people who would connect the dots and find the patterns. Messages would be embedded. That was not my problem.

They said if my work was good, they would let me keep doing it.

I had fantasies of art and life. Of mixing the two. Of concocting. Distilling.

Because there was no reason why, while in Paris, I couldn't write a masterpiece as well. Although I didn't call it that, of course not. Something of my own, that's what I meant. In my free time, hidden from inspection. I never asked for permission. I was made to understand, however, that personal projects were prohibited.

I knew someone who had a small apartment in Paris, not a garret exactly. His job was taking him out of the country for a while, possibly years, to Africa. I could use his space if I liked. I took it. I thought it would be better if I made my own housing arrangements. That is, I didn't want to be under surveillance. I thought if I was on my own, I might have a chance. That I might take a chance. The people in charge said I could live wherever I wanted.

Now all I have to do is get on a plane and fly. I know enough French. That is, hadn't I learned French as a child? It was one of the required languages in the past. I hope it will come back to me. I pick up copies of French magazines at the underground newsstand on my way home. And I see that there are still extravagant apartments in Paris with high ceilings and silk curtains and baguettes on marble counters. Jake said I would not be living like that. All he had to offer was a tiny space in the heart of the city. But what else could you ask for.

I said Paris was just one place, among many.

He said think of the twilight.

PAINT CHIP

EVENING ROOM

twilight firefly:
tiny lantern for reading one
poem

neighbor's noise like crickets
in the floorboards: persistent
existence.

ACCOUNT 18

NOVEMBER 4

Existence is different in Paris, that's what they promised. I should be happy/grateful. That's what my contract specified. They also guaranteed me jewelry and food, in addition to money. The amounts are impressive. That is, irresistible. And so I take it all, including the black jade, the most precious stone at the moment. The stones are among the things that I cannot tell other people about. I cannot talk about my work. I cannot reveal my compensation. Jewelry must stay in the safe and shouldn't be worn except in extreme cases. I cannot discuss my particular genre of existence. Or my word counts. Or my conditions of experience.

I agree to all of this and more.

Their outreach is worldwide, which I am told is a bonus. There might be places other than Paris.

I agree to their terms.

And so: I write some stories. Is this a test? They seem so slight.

But things accumulate, do they not? That's what they ask me, and I say yes.

I feel like an assassin for hire, although they say that such a comparison is not correct. I have dyed my black hair pink. As requested, as required.

PAINT CHIP

ANTIQUE GOLD

As required, I do my best in the flats owned by other people not
to damage the permanent features: walls, doors, stove where I
would like to stick my head sometimes, but that would be crazy
and so I throw

rugs and pillows, sometimes replace damask with brocade,
flecked with gold thread, set the personal Moroccan lantern at
an angle and make an effort in one rented square of space to fill
it with charming effects, talismans and serifs, pointing
    the way, further in

until it's time to move again and I try to leave

a good impression
on another stranger
of another stranger
    startling
architecture.

OCTOBER 1

Architecture is not a problem. Housing will be provided, if I require it. I tell them I can find my own place. In addition, I will be compensated with various accoutrements. That's what they are calling things.

My employment conditions require me to give up all extra writing now, even in private. They cannot risk it. Even the most inconsequential documents have problems. I pretend to agree. But do they really expect me to follow such fine print? My micro memoirs are too small to be seen. That's what I believe.

Although they have spelled it out for me: sacrifice of personal life is required for this job category. Nothing new, nothing unusual. People have been accepting contracts like this for centuries. A lot of people would kill for this opportunity. This is my chance. To achieve my dreams, they tell me. And I think they are reading from the wrong script. But I don't argue. I sign the first contract and provide my fingerprint. There will be more forms to follow.

After they leave, I sit by the window.

I watch a man blow bubbles on the street corner. While a

woman arranges three white candles on her windowsill. She lights them, periodically. Once in a while, she drinks a cup of coffee. Or something else, looking out. Hard to tell. From this angle.

I have a new velvet chair that I sit in by the window. A Moroccan lantern from a fake souk in this City of Semblances. I have used their money already. *Luxe, calme, et volupté:* that's what I tell them, but they do not understand what I am talking about. Even though they speak French proficiently. I have heard them in the stairwells.

There is the hint—no, the promise—of travel. There is talk of other places. That's what they say.

PAINT CHIP

SOUVENIR

They say the city is always changing, but I don't know, New York always seems to be the same to me. I have an ancient black-and-white postcard of the midtown nighttime skyline that is slightly worn around its rounded edges, and the city doesn't look that different from today, frankly. Stark, sparkling.

I bought this card in one of those secondhand bookshops that used to cluster around Fourth Avenue but were mostly gone by the time I arrived. Still, there were a few left, and they sold not only books but also old prints (torn from books) and junk and ephemera. Bullfighting posters and Japanese calligraphy. When I bought this postcard, I thought I'd frame it and hang it up somewhere in my apartment. But I didn't. I already lived within the world captured in this photograph and I didn't need a reminder of it. I was in one of those tiny windows that made up the city (although you certainly couldn't see my studio, somewhere down near the ground). So I put it in a box. Moved the box around with me and then, one day, took out the postcard (which I was happy to find, having forgotten about it) and propped it up on my makeshift desk in London. No, Paris. I almost forgot what I was talking about.

I had moved overseas all of a sudden.

Where I didn't know what to expect to find, but I expected to find something.

Where every evening, I could look at my tiny vision/version of New York City and imagine how fantastic it would be to live there. I remembered the rush of electricity or whatever it was through the intersections in the summer. The shimmer across the asphalt at cross streets. The beauty of fire escapes. How a storm flung a ribbon around the horizon, past the corner to catch someone clutching velvet on the sidewalk, as gates crashed over storefronts. Pigeons scattered and lovers smudged the bricks with smoke, some crimson, then refused to share their bright ideas with the man reading an old hardback in a taxi that sparkled like a momentary canary yellow diamond stuck in the pavement-tangled twilight,

closing,

clasped.

SEPTEMBER 5

Clasped together, the first folders of instructions are presented to me. Printouts, no electronics. Too risky for the initiation events.

They say my task will not be difficult. The words will be easy. They mention an amount of money and some other things that will come to me, if I do everything right, and I say fine. This is what I want. This is what I wanted, that is.

I will be writing in the genre of crypto-reportage.

I've never heard of it, but it is all around us, if you look for it. I will write about urban life and evocative moments. Weather reports. Observations of street corners. Write to the grid. The blocks of text would have sides of equal length. Facts can be trimmed. Things might have to be invented. We'll see. But make things fit. Make things work. Very short pieces. But they will contain the code of something greater. (They call me a contributor. I will have a voice in this world. But no name. No attribution, rather. That was the beauty of it. That's what they said.) Hidden messages will sometimes, maybe, be found in my stories. But even I won't know what they mean. I am not sure how to embed information that I don't have, but they say not to worry. They have editors for that. My work would be in the service of a higher purpose, even if I didn't know what it was.

Another thing, however. In addition to writing what they want, I also have to stop doing my own work. They need to limit my outlets. So I have to give it up, my private writings. How do they even know about that?

They have seen me. I have a habit of sitting by the window. They know that I write, sometimes, in the evenings. They mention desire and ambition. They know about my micro memoirs, but they don't call them that.

Now, however, I have to concentrate. On my new career. On the one right way, that's what they say. The path to success. I have to stop everything else. Because texts could be put together in ways I never intended. I protest. But they don't want stray vectors of information, of transmission. The confusion of forms is conducive to decay. I don't know what to say. But I consent. They ask me certain questions to which I can answer only yes.

ACCOUNT 15

SEPTEMBER 2

I can answer only yes when they enter my apartment with an ultimatum. The row of locks on the door did not stop them. They move around my studio, which is in a former power plant converted to housing for starving artists, but only those with potential. I am lucky to have this apartment.

They cut holes in my walls, something that I did not expect, to check for things that they cannot name.

They sit down on my chairs, and someone breaks one. I apologize for its insubstantiality.

They have come to me because they thought I would be perfect. For a certain job. They have watched me from afar. And so far, I have produced nothing of consequence. That's what they want. I am worth more than I realize, someone says before someone else tells him to be quiet.

I think of refusing the work, now that they are here, in my apartment, filling it up with their dark forms. But they convince me. They mention the revolution. The newfangled warfare and pockets of rebellion. But the news has been full of such reports for years. I say it doesn't scare me. They say it doesn't matter because that's not why they're here.

The time has come, they continue. And then: Do you want to die now, in this hovel, in the middle of your prime number? Or do you want to live to be an old woman, sitting by a window, watching the city dissolve through cataracts. Everything: so beautiful.

They had been programmed to change their speech patterns, depending on the demographic. And when they phrased it like that, I did not want to die at all.

PAINT CHIP

PORCELAIN

I did not want to die at all in the middle of this Paris afternoon when the rain rushed through and all I could think was: Venice. Where people sipped cool pink wine among the canals and puddles, ignoring the smells and disturbances. I remember trying to find my way through the thicknesses of stones and trinkets and fish markets on bridges. It didn't matter if I turned the wrong corner. I was a visitor. On a journey to find something special that no one had found before. What crevice to investigate next? And is it possible to follow the standard itinerary and still make a discovery?

I wondered. I wandered, pretending to be an explorer.

I looked into a boutique that felt like a museum. Scarves of pleated silk and crushed velvet highlighted by spotlights. Citrine yellow, sky blue topaz, the best possible pink.

Then into a store fluttering with paper. There were also glass rings the size of hockey pucks, with gold flecks. Or streaked with silver to look like the sunset through the streetlights lining the Grand Canal.

Next door, eggplant was being grilled with olive oil and oregano and spread in see-through slices over wood-fired pizzas. People were drinking thick and sweet espressos in tiny cups. Saucers clinked with their satisfaction.

I went to Venice because I didn't mind getting lost in the dusk, among the things that were inadequate or stinking, for a while, for an afternoon, or an evening because there was a reward waiting. Something tangible—good as glass, delicately hand-painted—at the end of my journey. Something to take away. A souvenir around the corner. And then it doesn't matter if you're not the first person to find it, if you have to share your love with thousands of others, laughing, loitering, arriving at different hours, in other seasons. Venice makes your dailiness a special occasion. As if you were always on vacation. I try to remember the feeling.

ACCOUNT 14

SEPTEMBER 1

I try to remember the feeling, what it felt like when I got the call. The calling, they said. An assignment that I have to take. I should have been expecting it. And although I would never say I had no choice, the caller did make it clear that it would be to my advantage to do what they asked. Because there were things they could do for me. Or had already. My new apartment hadn't just fallen into my lap, for example. I am not as lucky as that.

I agree to do whatever they want, whatever work they have. I am ready for a challenge, but they don't want to hear about that. No delusions of grandeur. They try to explain the situation. Whatever happens, it will be better. We both believe that.

They are offering me a chance, a way out. They don't say where or what. I don't ask.

They say that someone will visit me. There will be a window of opportunity. During which I will be required to be at home and ready for visitors.

I have been told to clear a space.

Someone will check to make sure my room is secure. So don't

be alarmed. I said I would do my part. Don't look suspicious. And in the meantime, I could continue. That is, I could return to whatever I had been doing.

I go back to cleaning the glitter in the floorboards.

ACCOUNT 13

AUGUST 10

Glitter in the floorboards of a new apartment. A collage artist used to live here. That's what they called her. Something happened. But it doesn't matter. I am glad to have a fresh start. Time to begin again and do it right. Concentrate on the work. Try to figure things out. Do a good job.

Stay off the fire escape, which is hazardous, beyond repair. Someone will remove it later.

I have inherited the artist's furniture, for which I am grateful. Also some objects she must have been fond of. Who can say. I keep everything.

I am given a list of things that cannot be fixed inside the apartment. Structural adjustments are not allowed, but cosmetic changes are advised.

ACCOUNT 12

AUGUST 3

Changes are not advised. That's what they tell me when I am awarded a new apartment lease. I cannot remove the walls. But I can paint them. But I didn't even know my name was entered in the lottery.

I have to be ready to move immediately. I say that I am ready now. I am eager to give up this scraping by, writing snippets, and scavenging items on the sidewalk.

I have dreamed of foreign travel but never of housing developments.

Now, I will have city heat and a private toilet. Among other things. I will be allowed to live, to continue living, that is, in the middle of the cosmos, the chaos, this Chosen City. What every person wants at this moment in our history. Glory is not possible without proximity. That's the motto of the foundation that awarded me this room. I am lucky, everyone says it.

I tape small squares of paint chips, all the grays, to the walls, to the ceiling. There are colors called marble and velvet. There is Venetian red, then cherry blossom.

PAINT CHIP

TEA KETTLE BLACK

Cherry blossom branches reach up and scrape the ceiling in my hotel room in Tokyo. The room is not large but neither is it small. The soothing colors of aqua and sage don't disturb the dark, dark wood. A row of dried leaves is lined up in sand trays above the bed. A giant screen plays natural scenes and soothing sounds. There is artwork composed of antique kimono scraps, compositions that you have to walk up to and look at closely to appreciate fully. Green tea ready to be brewed in a ceramic pot, then served in cups and saucers (but not matching, of course not). There are Japanese sweets (plum paste between wafers) that you have to construct yourself. There is body lotion that smells like orange rind. And the relic of one Oxford English Dictionary.

An oblong tray of dried fruit husks is arranged so that you can see it from only one position: lying on the bed.

And then, the view of the city spread out to the horizon. All circuits and lights and symbols. I don't understand the language, but I recognize a cobalt peony blooming in neon every few minutes.

I sit on the bed and look out, past the husks, into the night.

I sip green tea from a ceramic cup with a wooden coaster. Each thing on its own, to be appreciated.

At dinner, I have to choose my sake cup from a bowl of ice, and each cup is different: one rough and gray like lava, one etched Italian glass in cobalt, one delicately hand-painted. One has to look at everything. No two cups (or plates or bowls) are the same.

PAINT CHIP

SILK LINING

The same is true in Paris. There are so many things. I take advantage of the opportunities to see the neighborhoods and spectacles.

There are bullfights in the spring (not in Paris), and I go to see them.

And I've seen that the bull always tries, every fight, to find that safe spot in the sand that he believes will provide courage or some kind of dusty comfort when the time comes: the *querencia*. This place where one can be grateful: at least you're not a donkey painted to look like a zebra in Tijuana. He paws the ground until it looks like that stretch on the sofa where the cloth is crushed, where one always goes to sit down and read a book. A light bulb flickers off to the side, a flash of sequins, almost. But it's not enough to get up for and fix, not yet. One more moment, please. In the blank space surrounding 5 o'clock in the afternoon, triumph seems possible—it's happened before (bulls have been pardoned for their bravery; bulls have killed the matador). And it's happened more than once. So maybe. But then something else occurs, and one is forced out, all of sudden, to another place in the world, like leaving Arles for Seville, even though the sand is similar all over the ring: we know this. And so does the bull: you can't fool him.

ACCOUNT 11

SEPTEMBER 3

You can't fool him. The reader always reads what he wants. It doesn't matter what you write. This is what Jake says when he finds me. But I am not writing anything. In the cheapest coffee bar, reading a used magazine. I never write in public. And Jake has never seen me in my room. Behind the bars. As far as I know. Does he know that I'm not a novelist? He sits down. I don't know why. We had been introduced at some point, previously, by somewhat mutual friends, but I never thought anything would come of it. He was not the kind of man to mingle with marginal characters. He didn't have to. He didn't have time. But he did have an assignment, something freelance that he didn't want to do. He didn't say why. He wondered if I wanted the job. Of course. I was desperate but didn't say that. But he must have known. He asked about my credentials and I told him what I had. Later, almost immediately, I passed their test. Money, like magic, appeared. I could buy illegal peanuts and industrial orange juice.

I asked Jake how he found me, in a place like this, just like that. And he said not to worry about it. I said I thought he was a medical journalist or a scientific reporter or something more specific that I couldn't remember. He said he had several interests. He said my housing situation was about to improve. Things were about to turn around for me in general. And I asked him why he thought I wanted them to. But he only said: Soon.

PAINT CHIP

SHEEN RIVER

Soon, I will have to go back to New York, maybe sooner than expected.

But right now, life is lovely and violet, and I am in London, and it isn't wrong to say that I love it, for the moment. Is it enough?

In New York, when I was younger, there were fireflies on that fire escape that used to be my balcony, every August. One could sit outside in the summer and read, but I didn't.

Although reading is more important than writing, that's what I think. If you had to pick just one way. But I also like to think it might still be possible to do both, to include everything.

I heard experts on the radio say the shape of paper will last forever and in a million years, you can still have it, to hold—some book like a brick of charcoal. But the print will be long gone, of course, sentences served. And the swirls of customized fiddlehead fonts won't even be fossils. Not any longer. Any wisps of love stories once cherished will have been released, and then the

mystery. The mystery will not have been solved, and those se-
crets now will never be revealed. In invisible ink. One dark and
stormy night. When someone pretended to believe—remember?—in the luxury of both fantasy and science fiction. As if we
could have it all. Because stranger things have happened. To one
enchanted reader.

Although for now, tonight, to tell the truth, I just want to live. In
London, for a while, for a while longer, before returning to Paris.
Where I will live for a while. Longer.

ACCOUNT 10

AUGUST 14

For a while longer, I will persist, getting by with less. My furniture is dwindling. My paper plates are disappearing. I have stopped wondering when this sort of life will ever end. Have stopped wondering if.

The chance of a lucky break is decreasing. Why should my life be special? Why should it be different?

I am living in a time when being a writer is considered a burden, not a profession. There are other jobs from the older era that people still admire (electrician, barista), but writers seem more like rats than pets. Being a writer is no longer glamorous. It is suspect. Like being a bullfighter.

That is, I speak for myself. And what else can I say. I shouldn't complain. At least I am not a painter. With all the fumes and expenses.

I could have been anything. That's what people said.

And books are dead, of course. People write projects or objects. Or something else. There is always a market for something brief (not poems, however). There are still commutes that need to be filled. There are still empty minutes in the night when there is nothing to watch, believe it or not.

I write my micro memoirs at night, but that is something else entirely, not what people want to read. (Everyone has an autobiography.) And they seem so slight: the memoirs, the evenings. I imagine something comprehensive later, something larger.

And then I have fantasies of another path. I think about traveling, as people always have.

Imagine Fez, Venice, Kyoto. Do they still exist? And the colors: red, periwinkle, pink. What about London, where I might be able to speak the language.

I write down the names of places and shades. One day, I will write something full of color. Not really a novel. And then I will paint a wall. Any color I want in a room full of souvenirs and things.

PAINT CHIP

PAPYRUS

Things like cat mummies, the falcon shapes, and the small curv-
ing coffins for a few snakes: these are the forms caught in the corner of my eye in the corner of the British Museum, when I
glance in the glass case to check my bronze eyeshadow, before I
move away, among the larger sarcophaguses with wrinkled linen
and a few lines of leftover gold smeared on cheeks, gold that was
once a sign that the flesh had become divine, according to my
audio guide, the treasure at the end and

more than mere

existence, and so I make a note for future reference,
    as if on a map under a palm
      as if I'd ever leave this city

even though gold, so burnished, is thin, as bad as onionskin.

ACCOUNT 9

AUGUST 1

Onionskin wallpaper falls off in strips. From my bed, I can reach out and touch it. I will glue the falling pieces back in place. Maybe, later.

My stove sputters. My coffee smells bad. But I drink it.

I look out of my window and see that someone has strung up laundry across her fire escape. Unadvisable. There are chemicals in the air at this hour.

I don't say anything and continue. I go to work. I make things to sell. Bracelets and cowls, bowls and pendants. I work in stores, off and on. I wait for things to happen in this City of Imperceptibilities. I do what I can and save important items in salvaged boxes.

Everyone has an ark.

That is, an arc. A segment of life to follow, from one end to the next. It doesn't matter how long, as long as it is meaningful. That is, productive.

At home in the evenings, I try to work, to write, but what is there to say. I see that the laundry outside has fallen apart, somewhat. I should have said something. Instead, I continue. To exist, to record my existence. People say: What's the difference. And I say several things, but they don't understand my sentiments/ sentences.

PAINT CHIP

PALM FROND

Sentences are lies! A man yells this to me in the subway, but I don't know what he's talking about. I try not to talk to him because I don't want to start a conversation. He carries a broken-spined book. He says this book does not know the secret of existence. Everything is unfortunate! He says this book is not the fountain of youth. I can't read the title. His book is twisted into an origami-like sculpture. Beautiful. And then he leaves, and I watch a wizard walk along the platform, looking into garbage pits with his wand. Outside of the station, on the sidewalk, another man blows bubbles at the corner of Broadway and Prince on this, his fantasy island. And I am not unhappy to have returned, to have been returned to this city of New York. This is where I, too, learned how to live and failed to accomplish something, eventually.

ACCOUNT 8

JUNE 2

Eventually, everyone feels it: the Impossible City is changing. The weather is becoming colder.

I came from elsewhere, like everyone else, during the season when sheets of ice fell from skyscrapers and killed too many people. I would have to be careful. I would have to watch where I was going.

And so I did, I do. I keep going, hoping.

But I fantasize. About traveling, about being. A ballerina in Shanghai or a pastry chef in Bruges. I imagine a fiction in which I am someone new, but I don't write that. Of course not. Who would.

I try to think of something better, something grand, something good. If only I could do it.

What if I never meet my quota for achievement?

I will wait and see. Keep an eye out. What else is there to do. Sometimes, I am confused. Too little food. But all the projects about hunger have been written. There is so little left. I need something new. And I don't want to die, not like this, not now. With all the rain and ice.

The cold is not invigorating, not even slightly.

ACCOUNT 7

MAY 2

The cold is not invigorating, not even slightly. According to the last report, the city will be cold from now until the end. Climatic readjustment. The seasons are not what they used to be. We have to get used to it. The recommendations say to stay inside as much as possible.

People don't like to talk about the weather.

And the neighbors are confusing. There are languages I don't understand.

I have found a new place. To rent, again. How many times has it been? The City of Changes. Everyone is always moving. This is the time of year for it.

My new room is better than the old one, maybe. It has a slightly larger window. I was told that prostitutes had lived in it before me. They painted all of the walls black. That's why the front door doesn't shut exactly: too many layers of white paint had to be layered on top. To cover it up, the black. The lock can be forced to work, however. I think I will be all right.

I found a scattering of artificial fingernails in the bathroom when I first moved in, but I threw them out and now I try not to think about it. Start again.

Things are progressing. Slowly. I pick up furniture from the street and rearrange it. Sometimes, things break. I clean the bathroom again and again, but the white remains gray. I use the sprays for bugs. I try to create a space that is secure and serene. Where I can both live and work. What everyone wants. The best of both worlds.

I watch the red squirrels in the pink trees through my window. That doesn't happen often.

I try to figure out what to do, what to write. I am still thinking about one big book, but no one publishes books anymore, only projects. I have to remember what to call it. Especially in public. Although, I don't talk about things like that.

I look out onto the gardens of other people, living below me, people who can afford the ground floor and that bit of land out back. They can't see the skyline from down there. But neither can I, stuck in the middle of the building, in the middle of the block. Penthouses are for people I can't understand.

PAINT CHIP

MUSTARD YELLOW

People I can't understand are living alongside me now. Different circumstances but the same city. One of the first things I noticed when I returned from Paris was the line of wheelchairs outside the senior facility. I don't remember the old people from before. Maybe they've just arrived, or returned, as I have. Maybe they were trying to be invisible but have given up the effort. Because now there are rows of them in dirty ochre crocheted throws. Every one of them in a wheelchair and watching the passing traffic in silence. The quietest people. That's why they're allowed outside. They have accepted their situation, and they confront their reality with equanimity. They don't care if it rains. They never throw things at pedestrians or harass the dogs that have to be walked. Dogs always walking. The same circle and loop. You'd think dog walkers would get tired of it. But in the latest poll, people said that dog walker was the job they fantasized about the most.

Two dogs: one stops to smell a smashed mouse while the other barks at umbrellas opening up like wet petals, and I remember the metro, another country. A crowd of tourists surges, and someone urges two dogs to move on, to learn some lessons, while struggling to hold on to leashes in the middle of thunder and storm sticks like glitter to fur and sweater. Try to love another afternoon as if it were a Frisbee, a freebie, even if we've seen it all before. A greyhound might appear around the corner and look: someone has left a trail of watermelon chunks, pink tourmalines, most precious color, in the crosswalk, through the intersection of unparalleled streets: follow the path invisibly marked. Don't worry about where to throw the ball next. Don't worry about dropping it. Just catch. One yellow twilight. That has been walked.

PAINT CHIP

SALMON PINK

Walked through the streets again today, as always, trying to orient myself, to reorient myself, that is, to find some direction. Sometimes, I have to remind myself where I am. No longer near the bottom of New York but at the top. Sometimes, I try to remember where I've been. Because it's like a balm to remember, and I try to be grateful. There are so many things. I think of the lepers at the last colony, on that island, where they saved for later the coffee, quinces, crisp bread, whatever was brought to them, whatever they named, when the fishermen, moonlighting, arrived from the mainland. They took it all inside, through the tunnels of the island's fortress that no one else would ever have any use for and fortified the remains, where possible, with the partial things—grounds, crusts, shells—the gifts of leftovers stuffed into the walls to keep the chill out when winter came but meanwhile played backgammon, if they had a board, into the long evenings when everyone's summer was slipping, pink, too warm.

PAINT CHIP

OCHRE

Too warm and on a small boat. I remember that much. Sailing past Vesuvius with its green slopes and hot black streaks. Its crater covered with clouds. And at the bottom, slowly crawling up the sides: the next Pompeii. But I couldn't do anything about that. While eating cashews in the cockpit.

In Pompeii, when the painters needed black, they burned bone

or ivory, depending on what they had, what they needed for their art—all those walls, still red and teal: they knew how to make a sacrifice, how to clarify, they knew what to do back then even if they couldn't believe a volcano

was true
and now

the museum is full of lessons with objects (raisins of gravel) even though I can't read the captions, like omens in Italian, too brief,

on onionskin paper in cabinets before escaping onto the sidewalk, almost dark, where someone might take a hint, buy a print,
there's still time, and paint the larger picture: cracked

cups of coffee, charred pizza, bright windows filled with over-
flow bottles of fluorescent yellow limoncello.

NOVEMBER 20

Limoncello: a surprise shipment, but what is it? It doesn't matter. I just have to shelve it. The bottles are heavy. The labels are unreadable.

The flash job appeared this morning, and I took it. Now I am in the middle of aisles of blank spaces to be filled in. I don't know enough to do this job properly. But I will do my best. I am staying here until it's finished.

This will buy me time, which I can spend later. Back home, in my hole. That's where I want to go. Where there is an infestation of some kind in the bricks. I sometimes see tiny eyes through the chinks. But if I keep the lights on, they leave. Then I can work. That is, I imagine I will. I will start to write something. Something that will require me to wear a black organza skirt one night in my future. At least one night in my life.

People that I work with ask me: What is your story? And I have to say something. But I don't know what. I need a hook and an anchor.

I don't mention the micro memoirs, of course. I don't want to be investigated. Also, that's not even a real category. So I say other things. I say: one day in the future. Or: I don't like to talk about my work. Maybe: a manuscript in progress. And they say: Like a book? And I say yes. I don't know if it's the truth.

I imagine a handful of nice lines, stacked up, spaced out, just so, just right. Something that might get picked up.

Although I have no network. And no circle. I am not part of the grid that runs things, through which information is transmitted. I know it exists. You can feel the vibrations.

PAINT CHIP

CARDBOARD

You can feel the vibrations come up through the sidewalk, from the subway, that's what I think it is, but who knows if that's what it really is, and I just keep walking.

Sometimes, I have to get out of that glassy fantasy apartment filled with forest candles and zebra orchids, although I love it, of course. Someone knew, for the most part, what to put in, what exactly would convince me. *Luxe, calme, et volupté.* Maybe I was the one who made those decisions.

Today I saw two men in mango ties take a break at lunchtime to sit on the steps of a museum. They blew smoke into the air. The money, one said, is the main thing.

ACCOUNT 5

NOVEMBER 2

The main thing is to keep going. Don't stop to help anyone. That's what the reports say this morning. Don't go outside if you have a choice. Don't go to work unless your job is critical. There is a record low for cold weather.

The Shimmer City is slick with ice.

I brush the snow off the inside of my windowsill.

And I do my best, that's what I'll call it, later. I won't talk about struggle. Because other people have it worse. I know that. But other people also have it better. They live in penthouses above me. They light candles even though they have electricity.

I think ahead, to a magical time like science fiction when something happens and I am in a different place, a better position, maybe. That's what I think. I look around. My fate is in my hands, that's what people say. And the cold is no excuse for not writing. Neither is the lack of money or topic.

I know what I have to do.

But I don't do it.

But I want to.

How many drafts will it take?

Some things take forever.

It would be better to want something else. Maybe. I can't decide. I go through the list of all the things that other people have/love.

PAINT CHIP

IVORY COAST

Love has dissipated, somewhat, almost, for several things. For the old books I used to find on the streets. Or the ones I bought for a dollar in those stalls outside the store. Also, I no longer need filigreed gold jewelry. Or stationery, which I used to collect from shops and steal from hotels. Because no one writes letters any more, of course not. I try to remember what it was like, the feeling of a heavy paper with a deckled edge. Or the sweep of a peacock feather painted along the margin. An elaborate monogram letterpressed into persimmon card stock.

I always looked for paper whenever I traveled. Paris, Florence, Thailand. And then I kept everything flat and unwrinkled in boxes. I waited for the perfect occasion to send a specimen out into the world. Sometimes, even now, I tack an example above my white lacquered desk. A reminder to see something, say something. In the past, I loved the thought of writing one good letter but always hated to disrupt the beauty of a particularly nice piece of blank paper. What if I made a mistake? Those were the days.

PAINT CHIP

SMOKESCREEN

Those were the days of wandering around in various cities of haze and golden dust. Things were just coming into focus. In Athens, I watched a woman tell a child not to touch the dead dog, legs up, at the base of the Acropolis. Because who knows what happened last night, or even before that. And the child said, all right, of course, but he went back to look while his mother gathered up the things of her world, dried thyme and blue pots, candles and zucchini. Things that he would have never considered. She bought one long black shawl from the stalls and thought that her child had learned his lesson. About which things were to be avoided (and cherished). And so she never discovered that he was lagging behind, bent over like an old man too close to the brown fur as dry as grass in this summer, ready to burn. When he said to himself, or asked, something ancient and unhurried. And in a foreign language.

PAINT CHIP

GRAVEL

A foreign language leaves me, and I can't figure it out, that is, remember, the Japanese, but then a sign, I can almost see it. The
sign said no photographs. Of the rock garden, where each stone
is silver, difficult, a lesson, people think, like a snowflake, then a
whisper, but no, reconsider: something graver in their number of
perfection: fifteen mountain slivers slightly blue

placed
    just so

you can see at best only fourteen, in the winter, even as we move
and make an effort, slipping in socks, to get a good view, on what
looks like lacquer, back and forth across the earth, between a
rock.

ACCOUNT 4

SEPTEMBER 12

A rock through the window doesn't scare me. That's what I say. I say that I am happy to be here, in this City of Consequences. When I first arrived, people (friends and relatives, miscellaneous collectors of personal information) said I should have stayed put, where I'd always been. Where certain things were dependable rather than impossible. Where the sun was still shining, for example. I said that change is good for people. Good for places. But in those days you could say anything.

I said other things when people pressed me:

Because I have to see what the city is.

Because I dreamed of it as a child.

Because it is the center of the universe.

Because I want an adventure.

I don't know.

Because I want a place to go.

I would like some room. One room. A room of one's.

Someone said I might be stranded in a cold-water flat.

But I said all that was in the past. I'd read about those struggles, in another era, when things were more medieval. Now there are codes and inspections. Someone said the old problems had come back but that I didn't know about it. It doesn't matter. I believed that I could live with cold water if I had to.

But I was wrong about that.

So I have moved, and today is the start, again, of my real life, finally. This time is the beginning. The other was just prelude. It took a while for me to figure it out.

I have moved a few things with me, the things I can carry. One coffee mug, a pair of shoes.

My new apartment is moldy, but that is better than other problems. The walls sometimes shake. I am told that having a weapon isn't a bad idea, but real weapons are hard to find. I could make something myself, that's what one neighbor tells me. He can show me how to do it. I say I'll be fine with a few locks. And he says, not quite. An apartment is not a diary.

PAINT CHIP

STRING

An apartment is not a diary. You cannot just look into the windows, even though they are open and uncurtained, and figure out a life. This part of town is difficult. But a display of cotton candy—all baby blue and soft pink and buttercup hopeful yellow—outside of a rundown steel-rimmed storefront stopped me in my tracks. And reminded me of something I overheard on the street, earlier, not recently, in another city, maybe Paris, I can't remember: Yeah, I just couldn't pull the trigger today. And I wonder what it was that stopped him. What thread he was hanging by.

ACCOUNT 3

JUNE 7

Hanging by a thread. Hoping to figure it out. My life, my work, both, together. Everything is difficult in this Explicit City: that's what they're calling it now. As if things were obvious. As if absurdity weren't an option.

I do what I can and try to live up to my promise. To fill my quota. But I haven't written anything yet, not really.

I walk around the city when the alarms are off and individual exploration is allowed.

I learn to navigate, even triangulate, when necessary. Extrapolate, maybe. The stars have been erased, but other things have not. And everything is personal, occasionally.

I add installments to my micro memoirs in the evenings as if my life depended on it.

But this is not the way to get ahead, I know that. But it's what I have.

I hope to start working on something else.

And in the evenings, I look out. Just think. I look out, through a layer of frost over glass.

PAINT CHIP

WINTERGREEN

I look out, through a layer of frost over glass, to see Christmas trees lounging along the curb, with whiskey bottles and pizza boxes, glad the holidays are finished. A fresh start is around the corner. You can hear the rumble.

A child in a stroller clutches a plastic bag of snow while his mother tells the doorman that she can't wait for this to blow over.

My niece wrote: I am polishing my snow globes, waiting for something to happen. And I wrote back: Don't crack.

ACCOUNT 2

APRIL 2

Don't crack the windows. They say to be careful. And the windows are fragile. The snow seeps inside, along the edges. The weather is unpredictable. I get up and shiver. Then make coffee, with old implements left behind when I moved in. Things abandoned by the people who fled the scene.

I take a shower sometimes, wash off the dust, in my kitchen tub, if I can bear the cold water. I will have to find another place to live. I can't live like this. I have been here too long already. Other people have radiators so hot that they have to open their windows even in winter. I have to change my life.

And in the meantime: what? A bit of work. That's what I call it. Boil some water.

I wrap a blanket around my shoulders and wear fingerless gloves. I hope that things warm up. Sometimes, the power failures come to my neighborhood, but I don't live in the last, worst zone. I am lucky. I write a sentence about how glad I am that I'm not a painter. Because paint is expensive. And so is the canvas, which is rationed. And the space to paint. You need a large loft so as not to suffocate from fumes. A writer can work anywhere, with minimal tools. How convenient.

But this is not quite right.

I can correct it. I have plenty of time to revise. Cut it, that's what is advised.

I put my pages in a drawer.

Enforce a separation between life and work.

Although I know that life is not worthwhile unless it leads to something. You have to go somewhere. Get somewhere. That's why I came here.

I will write something better later, maybe.

In the meantime, I think of other things. About being a painter.

In the meantime, I write in the journal. Write in the evenings.

Although the standard advice is not to keep journals at all. They could be used against you. There are certain professions I would automatically be barred from, if they were found. If I were ever found out.

I do it anyway. I write my micro memoirs, that's what I call them. I pretend they are fiction. As if that might make a difference. I glue paint chips to the pages. As if the paper were a wall.

I begin to hallucinate, to believe. That I can write whatever I need into existence. (Isn't that what writing is?) Maybe I would never have to leave the apartment. Except to forage for food and

fuel. Something to burn because it gets so cold in here. Also the
room turns black at night. Black as night.

    Writing

    down

    your fears

    erases them,

that's what I read in an outdated magazine from another era.

    But what I need is a handbook for how to survive.

PAINT CHIP

IRISES

What I need is a handbook for how to survive occasions like this. I don't like funerals, but I came to this one, I had to, some relatives demand attention, and now, in the tangle of dull jewelry and damp peach tissues, sometimes there is a reminiscence of women like her who made history: Savannah, Tera, and Udell. All their names saved in the white leatherette family Bible, unimportant to the preacher who finds our record immaterial and tells long stories by her casket about some other people.

And then, the slow ride to the cemetery.

Through the afternoon, with humidity.

Cars on the other side pull over.

Teenagers walking home take a moment. Even though they can see that thunderstorm coming.

One construction worker removes his hard hat.

And out on the grass, I open up my handbag, handed down, to catch those old silver dollars that old men still ask me to treasure (to bury).

How embarrassing.

Don't be silly, they tell me. There might be an emergency. In the city.

But everything is different in the city. I say there are meditations in an emergency.

ACCOUNT 1

NOVEMBER 20

In an emergency, no one would find me. In this City of Contingencies. No one tells me how to get out of the barred windows. No one tells me how to get out of my lease.

This flat, the first one of my real life. It is too small, too cold. Almost no furniture. Hooks on the walls for clothes. A tub in the kitchen that has no plastic shower curtain. Someone has painted over the old wood floors. It is in the British zone, part of the agreement with the New UK. I hope to leave it as soon as possible. To begin again somewhere else. My first attempt is a mistake. I have to go. But first, I had to start.

Keep moving, that's what they say. In order to get ahead. Everyone changes apartments as soon as possible.

But there are warnings. Reports of an upcoming struggle. It will be difficult for writers, among others. There are several professions that have been downgraded.

But I am in the city, at least. That is, they let me in. I passed the test for entry on the inspection island, after waiting for weeks. Out of touch. I could have been nonexistent.

The city wants people with vision, but no squatters. So how

to explain all the bodies currently living here in squalor and famelessness? They failed to execute their plans. It could happen to anyone. There was no way to verify someone's sincerity during the application process.

I, too, have a plan, copied from an old book, about what to do. How to be a success. Wake up early. Write it all down, but start small.

I will use the smallest forms possible to get started, following the Japanese model.

When people want to know what I am writing, why I am writing, I will say: something. Who knows what. I can't explain it. Or don't want to. That is, I am just writing what I know. Not to worry. But then, when no one is looking, I will write what I hope.

What I hope is to keep going. Until I can get ahead.

And if things don't work out? Do I have an escape route? No. I don't even have room for an inflatable raft. Not inside this apartment.

I look out. The stone walls are as white as paper. Everything has been sprayed. I can't see anyone else. All the other people. I can't imagine how they are managing. What they are doing. It doesn't matter.

I sit in the cold, on my bed, and try. To focus on a bit of art and forget this life. This city. The coldest autumn.

There is a tower in the distance, all green glass, but I can't see it. I do not even believe it exists. Not really. I listen.

The wind comes through the windows. There is a gap between the glass and the sill. I will have to find some tape or make some up.

I will try to make things up that sound reasonable. But also desirable. An alternative reality that people want to live in. The main character should not resemble your average reader. Should not be stuck inside an apartment with failure. Not stuck forever. There should be a way out. There should be a path, a journey, a bit of magic. I want to write something that everyone can read.

But so far, I haven't.

I stay inside my apartment at night. Keep a journal as a substitute. As a companion. Who would object to that? Just a stack of old-fashioned paper. But I keep it hidden, in any case. I know that much. Not to expose myself. I can abandon it later, after I have accomplished something. How many times do I have to convince myself: accomplish something.

PAINT CHIP

SILVER SCREEN

Accomplish something with your life! A man on the street yells
this out to me. He tries to force upon me a paper flower. The end
is near! A man on the subway says: abandon ship! A vendor on
the sidewalk says: fresh coconuts. A man on the steps sings:
America, the beautiful. A man selling jewelry gives me a poem to
read. It is written on joss paper from Chinatown, a rough square
of brown paper with a gilded center. The paper is more beautiful
than the poem, and I keep it.

PAINT CHIP

PINE

I keep it to myself, my last message of the year, of my life, season's greetings, best wishes, that is, I don't send out anything. Do people/readers need another gesture? I hope by now that everyone is self-sufficient.

The doctor said to expect confusion and fragmentation at the end. Nothing serious.

The champagne is fizzing and it's difficult to see through the blur. At least I know there are still things here. Both to be opened and to be wrapped.

I think of presents/presence and wonder: what's the difference?

Should I ruin the surprise? And how much time do I have?

Because this is not the death date I had in mind, the one that I had planned for, for so long, so long ago, the one that was going to be the reward at the end of the journey, for a job well done, the one that was going to bring me closure, this is not like that at all, but maybe it is close enough. I thought a proper suicide, at the right time, would be like the foil seal on a handmade paper bag in a Kyoto gift shop: the final touch. The thing that ties it all together. One fine body of work. But I don't have a fine body of work, or even a body at all, almost, not any more. I never wrote what I planned. Instead, I planned ahead. I persisted. I still do.

The star-flecked wrapping paper is flapping, revealing the gifts.

The sparkle of other buildings surrounds me. But there are no reflections. This city is something, but I can't remember what. This city of something. Whatever you want to call it. It looks like it goes on forever. I can't imagine not. And I have apprehended, momentarily, but then: what time is it? The sirens in the distance sound yellow. The flashing sign outside my window switches to Japanese to remind me.

That was it: that is, this is. Things are finished. More or less. No time for corrections. The night feels green, velvet. And there are no corrections, in any case. Only proofs. Yes.

ACKNOWLEDGMENTS

Many thanks to Margaret Luongo, Amy Toland, Eric Rubeo, and Jeff Clark at Miami University Press for their work on this book.

Thanks also to the following publications, where some sections of this book first appeared:

Blip Magazine: "Paint Chip: Smokescreen"
appeared as "The Golden Age"

The Boiler: parts of "Paint Chip: Spring Green,"
"Paint Chip: Nacre," and "Paint Chip: Silver Screen"
appeared as part of "City/Living"

Foliate Oak: "Paint Chip: Tea Kettle Black"
appeared as "The Way of Tea"

Glassworks: "Paint Chip: Silk Lining"
appeared as "Aficionado"

Mud Season Review: part of "Paint Chip:
Sheen River" appeared as part of
"Bookbinding for Amateurs in Autumn"

Tara Deal is a writer in New York City. Her previous novella, *Palms Are Not Trees After All*, won the 2007 novella prize from Texas Review Press. Her shortest story can be found in *Hint Fiction* (Norton).